BLACK THUNDER

An Indigenous young man living in a white man's world

by

JAMES WINDERMAN

Publisher:
Australian Self Publishing Group, Pty. Ltd. / Inspiring Publishers
PO Box 159, Calwell, ACT 2905, Australia.
Phone: 61-(0) 2 6291-2904
http://australianselfpublishinggroup.com

A catalogue record for this book is available from the National Library of Australia

National Library of Australia Prepublication Data Service

Author: James Winderman

Title: **BLACK THUNDER:**
An Indigenous young man living in a white man's world

ISBN: 978-1-923449-61-9 (print)
ISBN: 978-1-923449-62-6 (ePub2)

Prologue

The red and blue lights were flashing. Violent and blinding, strobing the streetscape. They were right on our tail. My mates were yelling over each other, demanding Jesse, the driver, take the next left or the next right. They didn't know where we were, let alone what was around each corner. Crammed into the back of the Ford Laser, my head kept hitting the ceiling with every jolt. If we hit another decent bump, I reckoned my head would be sticking out of the sunroof that this shitbox didn't have. We skidded and swerved, trying to put some distance between us and the coppers. To say it was cramped, with five of us in this small car and me the largest and lankiest sitting in the middle, would be an understatement. The two mates seated on either side were not big guys but they were agitated—hands, arms and legs jerking around, spit coming from their mouths.

Evan had a grand plan to get the cop car to give up the chase. In his mind, it was a completely solid and foolproof plan. The plastic toddler booster seat was thrown out the side window first. Then a pillow was jettisoned. Other crap—magazines, pens and cups—Evan threw all of it out. But no fuckin' way was that working. Fremantle coppers are never going to give up the chase. They're known for it.

Some pedestrians were out for a nice stroll in the early evening. I screamed at Jesse to not fuckin' hit them as he swerved all over the road. No way I was going into lockup for murder. We'd be put away for a long time. At this stage, it was just your average, everyday joy ride.

He swerved again and was doing a surprisingly good job of not crossing into the oncoming traffic. I screamed again for him to take it easy, pounding my hand against the back of his headrest. Evan in the passenger seat was sweating and grinning and drooling—whatever the fuck was he on, it must have been the good shit.

I gripped the pockets of my hoodie while trying to keep myself from falling onto my mates as we rocked from side to side. The money was still in my pockets. I considered chucking that out too but if I did, the boys would probably toss me out after it.

The Ford lost its muffler. We must have hit another speed-bump—hard. The resonating of the missing muffler came through the seat underneath me. Jesse was getting herded into a vehicle trap by the police. Another Fremantle cop car entered the fray, barrelling down and skidding and sliding on the asphalt on the opposite side of the road. Dangerous for them and us. A thought went through my head ... *are they allowed to do that?* I tried to swallow the lump in my throat, but my mouth went dry. Headlights were coming our way, directly in the pathway of our car. Surely, Jesse wasn't about to plough us straight into a head-on ...

Shit, what the hell, what did I have to live for anyway?

'Go, Jesse, go!' I yelled.

Chapter 1
JAILBIRDS

The screeching of magpies and crows having a red-hot go at it broke the morning silence. The mattress had sunk beneath my lanky frame, bugs crawling on my legs. Bite marks littered my limbs but it seemed I had grown a bit immune to bedbug bites in the last few days. A few dogs also slept close, and I'm sure fleas were hopping between them and me. What do people say? Lay down with dogs, get up with fleas! Yeah, well, it can't be helped at the moment.

The stale air felt thick and suffocating as the couples around me became restless from the noise of squawking and chirping birds. I was the only one without a partner, so I didn't have to excuse myself from under the filthy blanket.

I didn't bother to muffle the creak of the screen door as I wandered outside to light up. Smoking is expensive these days, but these came from a break-and-enter job at a petrol station done by a couple of the boys currently snoozing in the loungeroom. My parole conditions say I can't associate with criminals. But the people who make the rules have no idea what it's like for black Indigenous peoples in the suburbs. My Aunty Janice offered me a roof over my head. Who am I to turn that down? Parole can go and fuck itself.

Outside, I stood next to the beat-up Holden that someone in the house was using, and I glanced at the dusty side window-pane reflection with the sun shining, wondering who the hell was standing there. Yep, that's me, sucking on that ciggie as though I was running out of oxygen. I ran my hand over my three-day growth and considered if maybe a beard might suit me. Yeah, nah! My hair also needed a quick cut, and I made a mental note to ask Aunty Janice if she could do a quick job on it, blunt scissors or blunt knife notwithstanding. The only sharp instrument in the vicinity would be the knife used to slice the kangaroo tail open last night. Most everything else has been pilfered from Aunty Janice over time.

The birds were arguing about the leftover bits of gristle and meat from the elders' usual fireside booze-up. The stink from the cooked kangaroo tail still lingered in the air. As I stood and gazed around the place, I could see dozens of empty bottles, cans and silver wine cask innards lying around as the fire pit smoked away slowly, curling streams drifting up towards the scraggly trees and bright blue sky.

The dogs had followed me outdoors and were lethargic, hoping to find any tidbits of leftover meat. Their attitude mirrored my own, as I'd slept in the only clothes I'd been given from the shelter that housed me for the first night, and I was two nights into Aunty Janice's place, with no new clothes or underwear. I was just glad that what I was wearing wasn't green. I hated those prison greens. I might look (and feel) rough at the moment, but at least I wasn't in green. Finally, I had some semblance of colour—not green—back in my life. A couple of days out of the 'big house' and I was still finding my way: where to sleep, where to shop, what to eat

The op-shop down the road might be useful for some jeans, a T-shirt, and some decent shoes. As for eating, I've always kept a check on my diet by having at least some fruit reasonably often. So, the local greengrocer shop, run by a Vietnamese couple, might let me take some older discarded fruit that they probably can't sell. To their credit, they are well-known for helping people in this way. I'll walk down there shortly.

I could count eleven people in the room I had been sleeping in and another twelve elsewhere in the house. There were probably another six or seven lying about outside under trees and shrubs. Hopefully, they wouldn't get their eyes pecked out by those hungry crows while in a subconscious alcoholic stupor.

I was in Coolbellup, in the Perth region, close to Fremantle. Loads of Noongar people live in the area but I've never understood why they're attracted to this part of town. Maybe it's something to do with the state housing authority giving Indigenous blacks asbestos-laden basic houses, infested with all sorts of bugs. The houses no one else wanted.

Overcrowding is the new normal. My mob struggle to find decent shelter anywhere. My Aunty Janice is a godsend, allowing any of the mob to crash at her place anytime—no questions asked. Other extended family and general mob have been ousted by the state housing authority over the years—too much constant boozing, fighting and the eventual self-initiated demolition of the premises they were granted by the state to live in. Typically, a sign suddenly appears on the door saying: 'By council orders, this house is not fit for human habitation'. And that stuffs everyone around because within thirty days the place is boarded up and the locks go on, and that's another house that's off limits for some desperate people. But my Aunty Janice won't put up with any of that fighting crap, except for some backyard fireside boozing and maybe some small arguments breaking out ... but no violence.

I'd only been out for a few days after a two-year sentence. Parole got me out in thirteen months because I was mainly a 'good boy' while inside. On my best bloody behaviour, wasn't I? Aunty Janice immediately put me up and a good thing too—I had nowhere else to go. Just being in possession of these smokes would get me back inside if the cops were able to track the offenders down. CCTV and all that.

But instead, I lazily limped around the backyard picking up a few bottles and cans and throwing them into a pile. The bottles could be a real problem if left around—broken glass cuts into everyone's bare feet, and the old blokes who had diabetes couldn't afford that to happen.

More than one uncle has lost his foot or leg to diabetes in my short life, and cuts and infections only made them more at risk.

It's hard for a man in my mob to live past fifty. The whities in the hospital said they cared but their actions didn't seem to back up their words. They all went home every evening to a nice clean joint with a fridge full of food and forgot about the so-called dirty boongs that kept crowding into the emergency department of their hospital.

Not that there were many of us left to do any overcrowding. There are quite a few in the clink for a fair bit of time, and many more are on the path to six feet under. Wiping us out or keeping us out of sight seems to be the name of the game.

I took another long drag on my Winnie Blue and thought about what I was going to do with my life, now that I had one in front of me. The smoke burned as it hit my throat; I had a burning feeling in my mind, thinking about the choices before me. What path to follow? What choice do I really have? Is my life over before it started? In the 'big house', there weren't many choices or decisions to make, and that became habit. Now I'm out and I have to decide what to do.

It took sixty seconds before my anger got the better of me. It usually did these days. That's not good. I flicked the butt away.

My name is James but everyone calls me Jim.

I'm twenty years old, and an anger has seized me.

I don't know what to do or who to talk to.

My cousins are fuming. My aunts and uncles are deeply despondent. They're all drinking themselves to death.

The white mob have taken everything away from us, and they couldn't give a fuckin' shit.

What a fuckin' life for any of us. It's enough to make anyone weep.

Chapter 2
DRIVE AWAY AND LIVE WITH THE CONSEQUENCES

Life in prison wasn't so bad, really. It's just so fuckin' boring. And my God, you get sick of that damn shade of green. When you hear about interesting shit happening on the outside, it's bloody frustrating not being able to be part of it. But that's what the whole thing is about. Paying the price. Rehabilitating and all that shit. You're supposed to realise what you're missing. The prison puts on courses and talks that I actually attended, and surprise, surprise ... I actually learned some things. So, get this, we all complain about the prices of things in shops but I learned all about the tax system and how everyone pays their fair share to keep our society going. Supposedly, the only certain things in life are death and taxes. And wouldn't you believe it ... there are some guys in the clink trying to get out of that second one. They got caught, and look where they ended up.

I'm sure some people were disappointed in me for ending up in that place. I've never been a violent person and had never even come close to breaking the law. I had a good education. I was just following the boys. Perhaps that makes me stupid, and yeah, it was crazy to do what I did but mates are mates, and I just tried to keep up with them. What shits me the most is that people will just follow the stereotypes and say it's just another example of a black kid doing the wrong thing after everyone had tried to help him out. That's really fucked up and not the truth by a long shot. But in the end, the coppers had me by the short and curlies, and the evidence pointed straight to me and my mates. So, into the 'system' I went.

Prison was called the 'big house'. Good (but boring) food, good mates, clean water and bedding and basketball practice every day. They were the good things. There are bad things, but I won't go into them right now. But yeah ... the sports programs were pretty sweet.

I'm good at basketball, and my lanky frame meant I was never picked last for a team. I'm big for an Indigenous boy—186 cm. Mum had a bit of a fling with a US Navy sailor when they were in Fremantle port twenty-one years ago. I'm an only child. He must have been a tall fucker, and I inherited his lanky genes and his ability in the hoops game. Mum never talked about him much, only to say he was black, gentle, well-spoken, and had plenty of cash. Cash twenty-one years ago is the same as cash now for any of the Noongar mob. How the fuck do you get some?

And that was the problem of my most recent Hakea prison stay.

The boys I was with on that night were looking for some action. I generally tried to attend basketball training every second night at Spearwood but this was an 'off night' and the boys loved to just hang about in the park, seeing what would evolve over a Wednesday night. Money hopefully. To be honest, they didn't want to be at home (if any of them had a home) because of fights, arguing and general unrest. Couldn't play video games like all the white boys did (and bragged about) because if a computer was at home, it was either nicked in the first place or about to be carried off by some other mob. Most of us had a mobile phone but trying to keep up with even the cheapest plan meant that more often than not, you would ring a mate only to hear 'this phone number is not in service'. How does a Noongar kid have the cash, set up a bank account and arrange all the paperwork that is required? It is all basically a foreign language to most of us. So, we'd sit around talking about clothes and music. Stuff that American rappers were wearing and playing. Shoes and clothes were expensive. Way out of our league.

We were comparing shoe sizes while sitting around the park when a car pulled up and a white sheila hopped out with her kid. I could have told her she was putting herself in a sticky situation. The park is not well-lit, and we black boys merged perfectly into the shadows just like all the white cunts liked to stereotype. We black boys are so skinny we could turn sideways and hide behind a pole.

The kid needed to pee. Only a toddler but Mum just whipped down his pants and put him on the verge of the lawn. The boys immediately saw the opportunity of a quick hijack and some action riding around the block. I never liked the vibe they gave off in these situations. The adrenalin rush, the fuck you attitude, the we'll-take-what's-yours bullshit. They're my mates but that didn't mean we all had the same belief systems. I tried to speak up in the past when a handbag might have been snatched but I learned to keep my mouth shut.

They didn't even stop to think about the consequences, just practically ran full pelt at the car and jumped in. The keys were in the ignition. That Mum didn't have a chance. It was all over in seconds.

My cousin Jesse yelled out, 'mate, are you comin'?' I let myself think about it for a split second, then ran and jumped in. The biggest mistake in my life started right there.

I got the piggy in the middle spot of the back seat but at least I had a clear view of the oncoming traffic. I realised someone should have taken the Mum's phone as we screeched away from the park. I turned around and looked out the back. She was already on the phone and most likely calling the cops. The boys were whooping and cheering. I was in two minds but couldn't back out now.

Her purse was on the dash, and Jesse threw it over his shoulder and told me to look after it. He couldn't trust any of the other three. They would think it was theirs to rifle through. I tucked it into the pocket of my hoodie, my fingers clenching nervously around it. The noise was deafening. The over-revved engine, the whooping and swearing and the adrenaline coursing through everyone's veins. I was sweating. The car was a bit older than we would have liked but it seemed to run okay. As we sped off, Jesse's foot slamming down on the accelerator, it occurred to me that some of these older cars didn't have airbags. Jesse kept hard on the accelerator, and the engine screamed in response. The mental excitement button was switched on for all of us, and I had a few bucks of cash to splash in my hoodie pocket, in a white sheila's purse. Evan, in the passenger seat, screamed that we were looking at some serious Jack Daniels time tonight. I didn't even want to think about that sweet sticky drink going down my gullet while I was sweating and nearly pissing myself.

Time became weird as some things happened in slow motion and some things seemed to be on fast forward, but I realised we had only got five minutes down Spearwood Road when the red and blue lights started up behind us. The chase was on. Jesse was a great driver. The bloke could be a stunt driver for some action movie—he was that good. He was making the poor beast of a car drift and turn at his will.

Now all the boys were yelling and giving him tips on where to go in the suburbs. Jesse may have been in total control of the car but he never knew the best ways in and out of the streets. No doubt the cops knew the suburbs better than us with their GPS and shit.

The speed was cranked up again. The car was pushed past its limits.

Jesse took the corners, went around the roundabouts, and straight through the bollards of parks. He was doing well, keeping those coppers at bay. His only mistake was not seeing the car coming at him dead ahead. We were on a one-way street. He veered off—dramatic as shit—and the next thing I remember was the dust, and screaming coming from the inside and outside of the car. And pain.

Jesse had been thrown from the car. He was lying about ten metres from the car, not moving. The front windscreen had exploded outwards as all the bodies in the car had been thrown forwards, and it looked like Jesse had been the one to have gone completely straight through. The other boys and I seemed somewhat okay. We had hit our heads, and blood was seeping out everywhere. No one had seat belts on, and one of us was on the front dashboard, thrown half in, half out, all the way from the back seat. We were lucky. The four of us finally staggered out into the lights of the cops, and no one tried to do a runner. Evan told me later that he had his seatbelt on, the wanker. Fuckin' safety freak but I can't blame him. It saved his life.

I got done for being in possession of extra stolen items—the purse, which didn't eject itself from my hoodie, and I was caught red-handed. So, my court case would be a little bit more personalised, and I would get more time than the others. Except for Jesse. He was dead. I'd just turned nineteen, which meant adult prison for me. Was I ashamed? Sort of.

I did feel bad for my cousin Jesse. He was only eighteen and had been a good mate. I could see that the impending funeral would be tricky for all of the boys involved in this.

The funeral was at Freo cemetery and was a big affair. I was out on bail, with my sentencing scheduled in a month or so. There was a lot of howling and wailing. It was upsetting. A lot of people gave me and the boys the evil eye, but since Jesse was doing the driving, logic said it was his fault. We were just passengers. That's part of the lie we told ourselves.

My sentence was finally carried out at Fremantle court, and I was sent away for two years with parole. I'll never forget that day. I hung my head in shame.

The prison was full of people with lots of lies to tell. No one owned up to the crimes they committed. They all breezed over it like someone else was in their shoes.

Well, not me. I needed to own this shit and be done with it. From day one, that was my plan: own it, deal with it, and don't repeat it.

So, being incarcerated was not a big thing for me, and it generally didn't bother me. I had a plan within my punishment period, and I was going to stick to it. What ended up bothering me a lot though, was being called boong, coon, nigger or black cunt, wherever I went. On the prison football field and even on the prison basketball court, the other team tried to stick it to me, even as a grunt in my ear while tackling or a heckle on the free-throw line.

And now that I was hearing it, I started to realise it had been there all along. Maybe I had normalised it, maybe I had ignored it. But for some reason, now I was hearing it loud and clear. And I didn't fuckin' like it.

You could only take so much of that crap before all internal hell let loose, whether it be on the basketball court, the footy field or in a shopping centre. My anger boiled over now and then when others saw my skin colour and nothing else. Some pushing and shoving, typical teenager shit. But could I say they were racist comments? Or was I reacting to something that exists everywhere, and I was just being soft? Yeah, I got angry but I never got violent. Thank Christ for that because my term at Hakea would have been doubled if I laid a finger on that white sheila when we took the car.

Everyone stereotypes indigenous youths into a fucked up social framework. Maybe they've seen it all their lives and normalised it. But the anger follows, and then a response, which could be unhinged. When you think about it, it's just so sad for that to happen to a black kid coming through. What baggage to haul around!

I'm pretty sure I would just mind my own business if I wasn't being called a black shithead or being scrutinised when I walk into the deli for some milk.

Still, the issue of Indigenous peoples trying to get ahead in a complex white man's world has and still will be a difficult issue to solve. And probably not 'issue' singular but 'issues' plural. (That's my education talking.)

In my case, the more the white people talk about it and the more they feel guilty about all the harassment of blacks in the past, the more my anger simmers. Everyone's seen the photo from the 1900s. The one of tribal men in chains, in the Kimberley region. Everyone knows what went on at Rottnest Island, not 15 km from where I stand now. How the fuck do we live with that knowledge? How were my ancestors treated? Bloodlines are important to everyone, black or white.

Somehow everyone in this fuckin' country is going to have to come to terms with all that shit, otherwise there will be no healing for any black fellas or white fellas.

Some bloke in Hakea said all the talk by white fellas was just 'virtue signalling' and meant nothing for Aboriginal peoples. I don't fuckin' know what the fuck he meant but I do know that first nations peoples are getting very vocal, and that's even without the voice of the white man.

While at school, many people asked me about my views on the celebration of Australia Day. Should the date be moved or should it not?

Well, I reckon that we should try and solve a few more of the day-to-day issues instead of arguing over a stupid date. Talk about a distraction. While my people are dying of crap diseases and living short lives, maybe we should focus on those things and not waste precious time and energy chasing a date.

And I've got a few more views on Indigenous matters in the 21st century. My brain seems to be swelling with all the thoughts of my downtrodden mob.

How I got here in this backyard is a bit of a story. My story.

Where I'm going remains to be seen.

I'm not a vocal person. Many Indigenous people aren't.

Maybe I've got to change my tune a little bit.

I know how to debate an issue and speak clearly. Maybe I should use that.

I've had five great years at Wesley College under a scholarship program and graduated Year 12. I shouldn't waste all that.

Chapter 3
MY DEAR MUM

Mum was originally from Mt Barker in the southwest. She was only twenty-two when she gave birth to me. She would be about forty-two now. Mum passed away from what the hospital called 'alcohol related issues' about three years ago. It was weird, but the people in the hospital didn't know her like I did, of course. She was not a big drinker and often said no when people asked her if she wanted a drink. Mind you, taking a swill out of a wine cask after it had been passed around through everyone's mouths doesn't sound very inviting anyway.

She was a hard worker—an honest person. She had been brought up living in poverty where the houses were thin, and the weather could be savage. She had worked as a farmhand, a cleaning maid and a shop assistant before moving to the big smoke. She appreciated everything she had, and she valued life above all things. She also loved animals and knew how to ride horses. If we went to the Royal Show in Perth (and for me, as a kid, it was very special), the equestrian events were where we went first. Then to the regional expo tent to see the Mt Barker display. In a big crowd at the Royal Agricultural Show, we didn't stand out. We were just like everyone else, in the sun, on a public holiday, enjoying the events.

But no doubt she had copped some racism in her time. As a shop assistant in the southwest, she would have been accused of short-changing customers, pilfering products and skimming from the till. But to the best of my knowledge, she wouldn't have done those things. She would've absorbed the racism and got on with work. But incremental racism of that sort is destructive. It hurts, and I know all about it.

She made me go to school at Hilton Primary School. We had a statehouse there for a long time. We often had various visitors from the southwest and Mt Barker when they came to see relatives in the Fremantle Hospital. Mum was very well spoken and knew how to read and write—which wasn't a given for every Noongar person in those days. So, her application to the state housing authority would have been comprehensive and accurate. And at the interview, she would have come across very well. Her application for a house in Hilton was done and dusted, and she was in.

My early years were all about staying at primary school. Sometimes, a very significant AFL footballer originally from the Mt Barker region would stay with us for a few days while he was in Perth for a match, and I would attend school, gaining bragging rights. Most of the time, I reckon no one believed me anyway. Who believes a black kid?

We got all our vaccinations at the Hilton Community Health Centre. Mum made sure I was as healthy as any white kid. The school had a dental program, and they gave out toothbrushes and toothpaste to all the Indigenous kids to encourage them to brush their teeth night and day. When I was given my dental pack, I just smiled at the nurse with my beautifully white and dentally correct full set of teeth with no fillings or caries. Mum was very particular about those things. She had great teeth, and she knew all about first appearances and a smile when meeting people. She taught me well.

When people asked me where I lived, I often said in the Indigenous way—'ilton'—missing my H. Mum helped correct me and then I realised that when I said Hilton, they—the white fellas—understood me. Maybe that's just another unconscious act of assimilation that the white people had won. And maybe I'm getting too deep into the matter.

As time went by, I grew taller and started playing serious underage basketball, impressing coaches. Mum started to wonder where I would go to high school. Somehow, she talked to the right person, and I got a full boarding scholarship at Wesley College in South Perth.

That meant I had to 'live in' at the boarding house and could come home to visit on the weekends, which I did at the start. The boys at Wesley were great and all that but I did miss my own mob.

Wesley had amazing sports programs, and I slotted into basketball without batting an eyelid. The academic program was a bit harder but over five years, I toiled away and passed my year 12 exams. I could read, write, decipher fairly complex problems and tackle community issues. What was harder still was that even in exalted places like a private tuition high school, racism still existed—it just wasn't as obvious as on the streets. Some of this stuff is built in, like the bricks and mortar. Tough to get out.

I had talked at length about this with Mum, and she understood that I had to make it in the white man's world and live with the burden of hidden racism. When she came to see me play ball in the intercollege events, she could hear the comments when her boy achieved a 20-point personal total to help Wesley College win the game. Her boy doing so much and doing so well but still getting racially crapped on, merely for the colour of his skin.

And this was where her depression started.

The signs were there when I came home for a weekend, but I didn't see them. I was all wrapped up in my own little universe and missed the signs that Mum was not in a good place. She always showed loads of interest in how things were going at school but when I think back on it now, her group of friends had dried up, and she just didn't go out much. I did notice the house started to look a bit untidy but who was I to talk, being a teenager and all. I saw some medications on her bedside table and wondered what they were but I put it all down to 'women's issues'. She was of that age, I guess, and I just fobbed it all off. I should have sat down with her and asked.

It all ended with her drinking hard spirits that she wasn't used to, lying down to sleep and choking on her own vomit. I don't know the exact circumstances, but she'd been out with some hard, regular drinkers, and that was unusual for her. Whatever the situation became for her, I was angry about it then, and I'm furious about it now. She looked after so many people but when the time came for someone to look after her, no one was around. Not even me.

I was seventeen at the time and had finished school. Boarding was finished, and I was knocking around with my mates, day and night. Home life with Mum was boring, and I wanted to be cool with my mates. I just bedded down when the night finished, wherever I ended up. That's why I wasn't around when she needed me. I'm a selfish prick and a fuckin' idiot.

The funeral at Freo cemetery was massive. Mum was known far and wide and was loved. As a good speaker, after doing debating at Wesley, I said a few words, but I broke down into tears and couldn't get through without blubbering. The wake was 'dry' out of respect, and no one argued with that. When I get some money together, I'll get the stonemasons to finish her headstone, and I'll have to think more clearly about what it should say for her.

I started playing B-division basketball at Spearwood with my sights set on A-division and maybe even a draft into the NBL. For the time being, the state housing authorities allowed me to live at Hilton in the same house, with my Aunty Gail—Mum's sister—in place as my guardian until I turned 18. I still had some focus, and I had to keep my mind and body occupied.

But I knew my day-to-day anger was rising, and unless I did something about it, it would get the better of me.

Chapter 4
KICKING GOALS

Boarding school is sort of like being incarcerated. You must abide by the rules, eat what they give you and go to bed when they tell you. The only difference is that when you play or practice sports, no fences are holding you in.

My other sport of choice was AFL (Australian Rules Football League). Some people—Indigenous people—say, 'it's our game.' I've heard stories of original white settlers seeing the very first games played by tribal boys kicking a kangaroo skin ball between two sticks to score a goal.

Whatever the case may be, the AFL is ruled by white people and maybe not even by them. It's a major corporate event now and big business. Not only did I play footy at Wesley College, I also did an academic paper on the corporate side of AFL. The major question I posed at the end was, 'are we going down the same way as the American system, where billions of dollars are involved?' I got an 'A' for that paper. It made a few people think, and possibly they thought I had some brains in that black head of mine.

At quite a taller margin than my next Wesley football rival, I was primed to be a lead ruckman. I had to have stamina for running up and back on the field all day, and a leap that would get me up to tap the ball to my fellow teammate. Naturally, I excelled at both. And naturally, racism followed suit. The opposing side might have had Indigenous players of their own but they got stuck into me regardless. Someone must have found out my birth father was an American, and sometimes before the bounce down, they would call out in a fake American southern drawl. 'Hey Jimbo, have you heard the one about the KKK? They be lookin' out for people like you. You bedder wotch out mon'.

That sort of shit made me laugh. What dopes. Obviously, they failed history at their own school. But I could see they were having a dig at my skin colour to rile me. And that's racism, however it's presented on the surface. But there was no point getting angry on the AFL field, or your game goes right off. So, I stayed in the game, stayed the course and I would celebrate a win with my teammates. None of us ever dobbed on others about the racism, even if it was by the opposing team. The umpires were too far away to hear it. A sly smile here and a whack in the guts there, and it kept coming. It just kept coming. It. Just. Kept. Coming.

I think now, maybe we should have called it out.

Hiding it and holding it in is destructive, not just for the individual but also for the community and the sport. Nicky Winmar called it out at the top level, and I should have too. The private school elite football competition might not like that exposure but who gives a shit. I was the one copping it. Probably others too, even in other teams.

We were down at Macca's one evening after an away game. Normally, the bus would take us back to the college but a few of us stayed in the suburbs to relax a little. The western suburbs have beaches and surf, and we wanted to take in some of the salt air and beach atmosphere.

Some boys of the opposing team had walked in. There was no friction, just general camaraderie for all of us playing a hard sport. One of the boys from that group ordered a coffee. The attendant asked if he wanted milk or would he take it black? At that moment, that boy swung his eyes at me ... and there it was. Maybe he was going to make a joke, maybe he was just thinking about the colour of his coffee. Maybe he was thinking about fuckin' milk. But as far as I'm concerned, it was there—a reminder.

No matter the school, no matter the sport, no matter the feeling of a win ... a simple reminder that skin colour seems to matter. It wasn't his fault. He had been brought up in a society that separated people based on skin colour, however you wanted to look at it.

Living back at Hilton after school had finished, I was asked to be around elders living in other local houses and having their usual booze ups around the backyard campfire. I had to go to show some respect, even though boozing up just wasn't in me for a while after Mum's funeral. They had their commiserations to pass on to me about Mum, and I had to give them that chance.

All were friendly and happy to see a fine young man trying to make his way in the world, in the way of all elders, black or white. Some mob were down from Meekatharra, and they were real black-skinned. Some of them were relatives in some way that I didn't quite understand. Real tribal types, I thought. Some men had the scars of their initiation rites. Tough men, quiet men, proud men and finally, drunk men. Perhaps wasted men.

I found a connection with these men while having a small drink with them. They asked me to come up there to Meeka and do the men's ceremony. That's something I will keep to myself for a little while, perhaps later on and perhaps seeing everything in a different light.

There is no issue of skin colour here with these people.

My mob ... from the north to the south of a sun-drenched country.

✧

Chapter 5
MEN LIKE ME

When I stop to think about it, there are many occasions when overcrowding seems normal for Indigenous people. Uncles, aunties, cousins, siblings all seem to live a life that is crammed to the rafters. Possessions flung into front yards, bedding crammed under trees, old lounge chairs out the front and kids' toys permanently littered everywhere. Drive past and anyone would know it's a Noongar house. Why couldn't we be like everyone else? Surely that's what everyone craves. Just to fit in. Be useful. Try to be somebody who gets respect.

I remember an uncle participating in a project run out of the Hilton Community Health Centre. It was designed to help men do something useful at home, even if they were living there temporarily. The project leader helped the men grow their vegetables in the backyard. I remember my uncle picking a massive watermelon and bringing it into the house for all the kids. It was a wonder that it had survived untouched for so long but there was an air of respect. He was so proud to have achieved anything at all. I remember saying, 'what the fuck does growing some vegetables mean for any of us when everything is stacked against us?' My negativity was drowned out by hungry slurping and eager grins. There would be another time for that question.

The odds are stacked against indigenous men. They have relatively short, tumultuous lives that end badly. Badly, as in ending up on a kidney dialysis machine for the short time they have left. When I think about what Aboriginal men must have suffered on farms and stations at the hands of their white man supervisors, I get very upset and my head hurts as I calculate it all. Maybe they put up with it; maybe they earned their pay packet. But the equivalent white man earned more, got a better diet, lived a better life and a longer one. And as far as I know, it's still going on up north.

I realise I need to take action in some way, shape or form. My voice. My reasonably educated voice is valuable.

It was only in 1967 that Indigenous people were given a new status in Australia. Wesley College taught me all about that. I could—and perhaps should—have done an academic paper that ridiculed that decision or at least brought it to attention. After all, a status means nothing without ongoing support. You can't expect the whole culture of people to change within a generation. Did white Australia *really* expect that to happen to First Nations people whose culture had been around for thousands of years? Nah, surely not.

Alcohol consumption went hand in hand with the new rights given to all Indigenous folk. It had, and still has, a terrible effect on my people. I would take it away if I could. To walk past inebriated and begging First Nations peoples on the streets of Fremantle is belittling and wrong.

These were once a proud people who had an affinity to the land and all its creatures but are put into a lifestyle holding pattern that only ends with their unnoticeable death.

My thoughts tipped over into action one morning at Spearwood shopping centre. A charitable organisation had set up a table to gather donations for poor, disadvantaged children overseas. After coming from yet another overcrowded and unhygienic house, it was like seeing red. I suddenly didn't have control over that simmering anger inside of me. 'What the fuck?' I shouted. 'Don't you know that kids are dying only kilometres from here, in their own houses, because of atrocious conditions? How about supporting them?' I just couldn't hold it back, as venom-coated words spewed from my mouth. I was met with stony-eyed disbelief and a strong arm on my shoulder from a security guard.

I slapped his arm away and bolted. I was fast and easily gave him the slip. But my face was recognised. People attended basketball games in Spearwood, and I had some explaining to do.

I also had some hard thinking to do.

How could I support my mob while playing the game that the white man controls?

Could I do both?

How much did I love basketball?

Chapter 6
A MATCH MADE IN HEAVEN

After Wesley College boarding school had finished and I had passed my exams, the years became a blur. They're not completely lost, just blurry teenage years. Though my time in Hakea will sit in my memory forever, as I recall the ward buzzer to turn out the lights, the ward buzzer to rise and shine, and the bell to announce meal times, every day seemed like the day before. Thinking about it, I was a bit lost right out of high school. There was some work for cash, and some bright spots where I had a girlfriend. And then life really sped up once I found the right girl.

I was offered a manual labour job for a tradie doing concrete work in the Spearwood and Hamilton Hill area. He started at 7 am each day, so I had to be at his joint before then. Connecting buses were a bit of a problem, and initially, the cash to ride them was another problem. Some bus drivers were good and knew I was trying to get ahead. So sometimes I didn't have to pay and just boarded with a nod of the head in exchange for a free ride.

I did my best and the tradie, Dave, paid me well—if sometimes a little later than he should have. With cash in my pocket, I was able to do what every other seventeen-year-old kid did. Hang about, do a bit of drinking, play some music and try to find a girlfriend.

At seventeen, I didn't think twice about chatting up Chanelle, who was sixteen. She was also Indigenous and came from the Midland/Bassendean area. We met when the boys and I were in Perth's CBD one weekend for a free concert at Langley Park.

Oh man, she was beautiful. Out of all the girls we flirted with, there was just something about her; unblemished, silky skin and slim, lithe body. I towered over her. It was always a matter of jest among the boys about how we'd eventually 'do it.' In the end, it was just a matter of where.

Aunty Gail at Hilton was not concerned, and she was okay with Chanelle coming down to Hilton for a weekend. We met at the Fremantle railway station and caught the bus up to Hilton. When I introduced her to Aunty Gail, it turned out that Aunty Gail knew some of Chanelle's folks.

I was not in any way ready to be a father by eighteen but that's how that first year panned out.

We had a son.

I had to work, be a good partner, be a B-grade basketballer, be a respectful man to my elders and be all things to all people. But most importantly, in the end, I had to be a father. When I say the years became a blur, it was all happening a lot faster than I had ever anticipated.

I helped Chanelle with the baby where I could, and it was back to Hilton Community Health Centre we went for those needles that I had, not that long ago. My 'baby' card was still there, and it was nice to be welcomed back.

Everything was going smoothly until it wasn't. My basketball was off; I had more sick days off work than actual workdays, and I was tired. Really tired. Someone had called me a black boong on the worksite and I got pissed off. That sucked up any energy I had. I know I took it all too personally but if I had called back to him and said, 'shut your fuckin' mouth, you white cunt,' it would have been on for young and old, on the worksite. And fuck me, I would get the blame. That's the way it works for my mob.

The pressure had gotten to me and without thinking, I chucked a wobbly after work and started screaming about injustices and unfairness. I complained loudly about stupid white cunts and their racist shit. Spittle came from my mouth, and snot erupted from my nostrils. It was ugly. I was too loud and Chanelle was scared, hugging our baby to her chest. I grabbed a plate from the table, and it seemed to go flying all by itself. It wasn't thrown at her or anything; it was just thrown. But it came from my hands. Somehow, it skimmed the back of her head when she turned to avoid it. A moment of madness. That's what it was.

There was no physical damage. Just a whole heap of mental damage.

And that was that. She packed her things and our kid up. No amount of apologising would change anything. I was just like all the other Indigenous men she knew. Too angry by half. She was going home to Bassendean at seventeen with a baby and a failed relationship. I had turned eighteen but couldn't relegate fuckin' stupid racism shit to the bottom of the ladder where it belonged. And now it had cost me everything. You would think I would know better at that age.

No one wanted to hear about my crisis. I had to suck it up. I had to consume it internally. But it was eating *me* up, not the other way around.

I gave up work and started drinking. My cash didn't last long, and soon I had none. Chanelle got most of my government supplied welfare pay and fuck knows what she did with it. I decided to visit her, if only to see my son, who was also a 'James' like me (of course). I caught the train up to Perth and out to Bassendean and fronted up at the door. I knocked politely. The house had a bit of a smell to it but I put that down to baby shit. Chanelle let me hug her when she came to the door.

She didn't look good. Worn out and looking more like my older Aunty Gail than the Chanelle I knew and fell in love with.

I don't know who was helping her with the baby but clearly, they weren't doing much good. One look at my son and I knew there was a big, big problem. He was covered in scabies head to toe, crying and scratching madly. Chanelle was crying.

I knew there and then that I had to do something. I convinced Chanelle that I was okay with her, and maybe she could put up with me. I wasn't about to hit the ceiling with any anger management issues. Not now when my son needed me.

We visited the Midland Community Health Centre to seek their advice. It was simple in the end, a matter of completely smothering James in scabies cream and waiting for the condition to be relieved. It might take days but James Junior could not go back to the same conditions.

I convinced Chanelle to come back with me to Hilton, if only for the short time it would take to get James Junior over the excruciating, itchy scabies. She listened, and we went back to the same room as before. Thank God for Aunty Gail.

Some people will say that all of these problems came with the territory for Aboriginal people who don't know how to keep a clean house or properly tend to a baby with all that is required. Hygiene issues and all that stuff.

But shit, they've been doing it for thousands of years, so why do all the white people get up in arms about it. Not their fuckin' kid. And a mistake is a mistake, so let's forget about blaming anyone. We all know the government does like to overstep the mark at times, though, and a social worker did make a house call. She was generally understanding about it and viewed it as a temporary lapse. But our names were now in the system, and any future checks would be counted against us for child welfare purposes.

And that's another big fuckin' shitstorm that sits in my mind. Haven't the white majority learned that you can't take the kids off their Indigenous parents? Even the threat is real. It's certainly not forgotten. Some people are still floating around as Indigenous adults looking for their original parents from the Stolen Generation period. And now I'm in the mix as well. Christ, when will it stop?

And here I go again, taking things way too personally.

We played mother and father for a while longer, and I had to do some cash work. I played basketball on Friday nights, and that kept me off the streets. Chanelle and James Junior would come along to watch.

Everything was moving along as it should for a young couple with a baby under care.

Until it wasn't. Again.

Chapter 7
DOWN THEN UP

got dropped from my team in B-division hoops.

I was a good basketballer but the coach said he didn't like my attitude. Too much 'agro' or something like that. Apparently, I'm not much use if fouled off. Well, yeah!

I told him I didn't like the racism shit thrown at my every turn in life. But he said that until I got a handle on it, I was off the team. To give him his due, he said if he saw or heard it while he was a coach, he would come down hard on it.

Chanelle wanted to see more of her Bassendean family, and she and James Junior went back for a weekend. I was a bit cagey about that after the scabies disaster, but she assured me everything would be good.

She never came back to Hilton.

Now I was off the team, off the regular job and out of family life, and I didn't have any money. Aunty Gail was really good about it and said that things would pass and get better. Remember my Mum's attitude in life, she said.

I knew my education from Wesley College should help my prospects, but it all seemed too hard. There was too much weight on my shoulders.

The original group of boys I had hung around with in Hilton had changed, and not always for the better. When I had come to visit on those boarding weekends, it had become all too familiar to me. And now, when I wanted to see my mates, things seemed very different.

Drugs were everywhere in the community, and no more so than down in these southern suburbs, well away from the elite life of a private boarding school.

Evan was taking meth and some of the others seemed strung out every day with no spirit left in them. Footy season was coming up, and most of them would look to play amateur level for something to do but I didn't hold out much hope for them. Coming off meth and dope would be hard enough. They were bored and had nothing to do and nowhere to go. Drugs filled a gap. I was no preacher, so I said nothing.

I was never into the drug scene. Sport was my foundation, and it has always been good to me.

So, it was back to the two sports that I looked to for a purpose.

I bit down hard on any anger issues. I trained hard. I actually skipped a short season in hoops but broke new ground in footy. A new club, new mates, a new attitude and life went on.

The racism shit died down a bit. Maybe it was me trying not to absorb it.

The AFL at the elite level was going hard against any racism, and my new footy club called it out at every step. At last, I thought, somebody was doing something. How long does it take for the obvious to sink in?

Things were finally looking up, even in small ways.

So why did I feel the need to hang around Jesse, Evan and the crew?

Was it only about going back to the familiar?

Why couldn't my new footy mates fill the void? Who the fuck knows?

Chapter 8
DREAMING

In my school years, and then later in prison, I had dreams. They weren't dreams of sex or car chases. But I tried to hold onto them in the morning because I wondered if they might come true.

I dreamed of football and I was playing in a team that was made up of Aboriginal players. The coach was Indigenous, the mums and dads watching were Indigenous and even the kid who brought out the oranges was black.

What made this team special was that we played only the opposition footy teams made up of white kids. And every time, there was another white kid team. And every time we thrashed them good and proper. There was no grand final, just instant game day in my dreams, but another thrashing of the white team. Our football guernseys were black and red, and the red dripped off like a blood-red ooze. All our players were somewhat crazed and desperate. On some nightmarish occasions, a smile after kicking a goal was turned into a grin that was turned into an evil show of teeth that looked like a dingo's razor-sharp jaw line.

My role was hazy. I just kept running and running to keep up, and I was fearful that my mates would lose. I couldn't let them down.

No one ever woke me up to tell me that I was having a night-mare, so I've always supposed that I wasn't. I never woke up startled or anything. They were just dreams that kept coming back. Not always, just now and again. But enough to rattle my brain.

Those dreams must have meant something to me. Maybe it was my never-ending longing to be part of a true mob made up of just my skin colour. Maybe I wanted to scorch the football field with an unbeatable team of indigenous players.

But whatever the case, I can see now that my place in the world didn't start or end with Wesley College. It started with my ancestors and my Mum, being Indigenous people, and I needed to find my true place in the world and be happy with it.

One day, there will be an Aboriginal team in the AFL. My dream will come true. Indigenous players have played a huge role in the development of the game at all levels, and the twists and turns of a draftee Aboriginal player making his debut in the big league is something the whole country likes to see on TV.

Maybe one day ...

Chapter 9

SECOND CHANCES NOT TO BE WASTED

I was doing well, thanks to all the extra effort I had put in. I was fit, and my muscles were ripped. I wasn't smoking, and I could run an easy half marathon. My hair was shiny, and I had it cut in a modern way by Aunty Gail. A buzz cut on the sides and rear with a manicured wavy mop on top that I could part on the side. My clothes were clean, and my shoes relatively new.

All until that fuckin' night in the park. What a mistake. And it was all my own fault.

I'd had a privileged life, all things considered. Sure, Mum's passing away was a big hurdle for me but she had made sure I was on the right path.

And shit, it was only a catch-up with Jesse and the crew. Okay, maybe I shouldn't have been there. Well fuck that … no maybes. Own up to it James, own up to it.

No, I shouldn't have been there, full stop.

I knew they were doing drugs. And with drugs, everything is unpredictable. Why didn't I stay away that night? Put distance between me and any drugs shit.

That's the pull of the mob for you. I was not immune to it, not many people are. Certainly not Indigenous peoples. Mates, mob, friends, family, cousins, siblings ... we all look for a connection. I'm no different.

I know that I've got this bundle of regrets piled on top of my shoulders but I don't want my life to be ruled by them. I might do one thing that brings in more regrets but then I'll just have to do two things that lift me out of the hole. That's how I'm going to order my life from now on. Extra effort to get my self-respect back.

Some people say that we are a product of our past. There's some truth in that. But for us Indigenous boys, who are supposed to stand up for our mob, I look at the Indigenous past, and it's pretty bleak. That makes all of us a crazy, mixed-up product if you think about it.

So, what to do?

There's no point in becoming a rebel. There's no point in going out and committing acts of violence or property damage to try to prove something.

There's no point in hassling whities all the time. It proves nothing at all and only allows the stereotypes to be proven correct. I can't be like Jesse and the boys and think I can take what I want, when I want it, like that fuckin' old shit-box car that proved to be everyone's undoing. The prison is full of men who thought they were owed something and just went off and took it. In some cases that involved taking a life ... and God help me if I ever go down that path.

I need to take stock of where I am in the present moment.

Another saying I picked up at Wesley is that the arrow in life follows one direction ... past—present—future. Maybe that's the arrow of time but it doesn't matter. It's all the same.

That third one is a major concern of mine right now, and I have to get it right. My own future.

But the past, too, is hugely important for Indigenous people, and slowly we are seeing people sit up and listen. So maybe that will come good too. Not that the past will ever change, just the attitudes of people looking back on it. And that can become the future.

I've been out of jail for a few days now, and I've slept each night in an overcrowded house in Coolbellup, and it's not for me. I'm not into the smell, the bugs or sleeping with other people so close. Shit, even prison was better than this. But thank you, Aunty Janice, for the help.

As I stand here, savouring my second Winnie Blue, I know I must make some changes.

For starters. I have to give up smoking if I want to go back to playing hoops or footy. At the least, I have to stop smoking stolen goods. I can't mention any of this to my parole officer. If he asks how I could afford to smoke, then he would know I was lying, and that's a big problem. So, out with the ciggies.

And my language is not real good. My old house master at Wesley used to say that anyone swearing had a 'potty mouth'. He collected a dollar coin for the swear bucket every time you said shit, fuck or something similar. If you swore within one metre of someone's face, then the fine was five bucks. That stopped it in its tracks. Right now, I've picked up some bad habits from the big house, and I have to ditch them and get back to normal. All words about skin colour, whether it's black or white, must stop. For five years, I was the best-spoken young Indigenous boy in the state. I can get back to that and gain some respect on the way.

Overall, it seemed like all the Indigenous guys at the prison were completely unfazed by all the racism stuff. They didn't seem to take it personally, even though it could get very personal. They shrugged it off, and I know prison life is not at all representative of life on the outside but that was a big lesson learned for me. Shrugging all the shit off.

I want to be like that, for my own mental state. I need to get past it all, shake the anger off and get on with living.

I want Chanelle and James Junior back in my life. Except for that one stupid action, brought on by targeted racism and my personal anger towards it, I've never done anything remotely violent towards her. I need to show her that I'm not just another toxic Aboriginal man. That I've learned to control my anger. I'm not going to use any excuses to get me over the line. It was all my fault, and I have to own it and commit to never going down that track again.

I want to play my sports, and I want my family to be proud of me.

I could make it to A-division hoops, and the coach said he would investigate some trials in B-division again. Dave said he has some regular work for me.

People are giving me a second chance.

I want to live in a normal house and be with my family and my mob. Aunty Gail keeps a good, regular, clean home with no mischief, and I know she will take me and my family back again. I'll head over to Hilton after the op shop and say hello. I didn't want to hassle the lovely lady on the issues of taking an ex-con straight off, but knowing her, she'll be okay with it. And she's a good listener.

I now understand that I live in a white man's world with white man's rules. It's the way it is now and has been for a long time, even though many Indigenous people didn't want to accept it. My own son will be brought up and educated in this world, and I want the best for him.

I'm a better person now than I was before Hakea which is pretty unusual when you think about it. Go to prison—to become a better person! Go figure.

Some of my mob mates inside experienced what I called 'loneliness' while locked up. There were no deaths while I was in there but it had happened. We all had to look out for each other, and the value of true friendship is another lesson I've learned. Just by giving people a little support—it goes a long way.

And now all these people on the outside are looking out for me.

I know I can do it with their help. They're good people, white or black, and I will not forget them.

My Mum had given me the gift of a great education. I should do something with it. I want to help my mob. I want to make a better world for all of us.

There must be a way but without any anger involved. I've realised that for people to give me support, I have to ask for it first.

That's not easy to do but the shrinks in the big house told me there were support groups I could join. Yes, that's what I will do, for starters. Anger management, they call it.

This anger shit within me, it has to stop.

It's eating me up.

$$\diamondsuit$$

Chapter 10
Working through it.

Who can help me work through all this? My head still feels as though it's going to explode.

But maybe I should be saying, 'who can *I* help?'

Some people reckon the best form of therapy is in the act of helping others.

I look around at my friends, my relatives and even my acquaintances and see apathy. There is a disinterest in the world around them because it just seems all so fuckin' hard.

I get it though. For a lot of people, every day is a constant battle just to stay on their feet.

When I look around and see the news of the day, it seems that the whole structure of society seems hinged around a competition of different racial groups all trying to position themselves in the best way possible to be better off than the other group. This formula trickles down to a competition between individuals of different racial backgrounds, sounding off against each other, and it can get very nasty ... the fundamentals of racism exist from exactly that starting point. There can be a lot of time and energy wasted on something when it doesn't have to be that way.

That's what I believe, anyway. I know people are tribal up to a point but we're all humans, and we have to behave better than feral animals. Nothing wrong with being kind to one another.

Coexistence seems obvious to me, and if we take the time to care about this shit, we will all get better at living life in the best possible way.

I know I look at everything a bit too hard.

I do too much analysis and delve too deeply into things. But hey, I can't help being a 'thinker', and some people would say we don't have enough thinkers getting around.

Maybe I've got some powerful Aboriginal blood in me, and it wants to break out. I'm thinking that's because Indigenous peoples have been carers for generations—carers of the land, carers of the animals and even the carers of mystical and spiritual beliefs. We've got it within ourselves, and no amount of racial bullshit will take that away.

And the way we are living—for both black and white peoples—it just seems so shallow if we keep criticising each other based on ancestry. I'm sure I'm not alone in this thinking, and there might be more to it, like who owns what land, who has rights to work on certain lands ... all of this and more will come up in our complex modern world.

But there is no reason to exploit one mob and get rich doing it. And then, if that mob complains, to criticise them for standing up for themselves ... no, I don't like that, and I will rally against it if I can. And I will help other people rally against it.

I'm just a young fella toying around in my head with these issues. It's important to me, as I work my way through them, to get into the mainstream of life.

I don't want to be just another pisstank who gave up on everything because it all got too hard. And as for the drugs, well … that is a very slippery slope and I'm not going there.

Many, many black people ultimately gave up hope. It's sad. I can't change the past but if I can add my voice to the discussions in a positive way, then I will.

So, we all move on with life and try our best. We take in our history, look at where we are now and plan for the future. Hopefully, we will get it right. Just try not to shit on people along the way through, and maybe stand up straight and be honourable to yourself and others. Maybe help people if they need it.

The people who have hurt me in the past, I don't pass judgment on them. I forgive them, and I'm okay with that.

All the personal racial crap thrown at me; I am slowly letting pass through my mind without sparing any precious energy analysing it.

And as for myself, within myself, if I have hurt people with my words or actions, then I hope that those people might forgive me too.

None of us are perfect, and we all make mistakes.

There is a key to life, and I reckon I've found out what it is—self-help and helping others, for starters.

I crushed out the cigarette under my bare heel. I felt no pain.

My anger subsided, and I got it under control. I can do better.

The birds have fucked off—sorry, flown away—and the sun has now risen in a bright Western Australian morning.

I *will* do better.

✦

Epilogue

This is not a story about an evil murderer or kidnapper.

Nevertheless, there is a 'thing' out there that follows me, and it's just as bad.

You can be kidnapped by a belief system that comes out of pockets of anger and hate.

It sleeps; it awakens. It hides and it exposes itself. It runs of its own accord, and sometimes it takes great personal energy to reel it in. It has its own agenda.

It is the big **R** word.

Racism eats away at your soul. It destroys your relationships.

It digs into the inner core of you just like a knife thrust into your stomach. And you bleed.

You bleed tears and angst and hurt.

You try to protect your loved ones from it.

It is a fire-breathing dragon settled into the hearts and minds of otherwise normal people.

It does its dirty work from the tongue, a policy, a written sentence or a simple glance.

But it is not all-powerful. It can be controlled. It can be weakened.

Forgiveness of self and others is the solution.

Small steps in the right direction.

I know all about it.

✧

About the Author

James Winderman is the pen name for Colin Scott who is a non-indigenous person living in Perth, Western Australia. Colin has experience in working with Aboriginal people and has seen his fair share of racism in his life.

He expressly wanted to help people (especially young people) understand the ramifications of incessant and incremental racism in society and hopefully help to prevent it.

Some of Black Thunder actually happened and some of it is fiction.

He hopes it is relevant reading to young people living in today's complex world.

I acknowledge the traditional owners of the Wadjak boodjar (Perth land) that I stand on at Derbal Yerrigan (Swan River).